Kathy Henderson

Illustrations by
Paul Howard

WALKER BOOKS
LONDON

For the long-suffering
residents of Woodland Rise

First published 1992 by Walker Books Ltd
87 Vauxhall Walk, London SE11 5HJ

This book has been typeset in Sabon.

Printed and bound in Great Britain by
Richard Clay Ltd, Bungay, Suffolk

British Library Cataloguing in Publication Data
A catalogue record for this book
is available from the British Library.

ISBN 0-7445-2407-5

CONTENTS

When's Winter?

Jim was fed up.

"When's winter?" he said.

"It's now, silly."

"Well, where's the snow then?"

"There isn't any."

"But there's got to be snow to be winter, and there isn't any, so it can't be, and that's boring, and I'm fed up."

Jim's sister Lizzie didn't mind. She was busy with her science project.

Jim's friend Arthur didn't mind. He was into mud and there was plenty of that. And the grown-ups didn't seem to notice. They just carried on as if it didn't matter.

But Jim minded and Jim moped.

"Well, you'd better get used to it," said his mum. "Sometimes we don't have snow for years and years, I mean when can you last remember any?"

"I can't," said Jim. "That's what I'm talking about. When's there going to be a *real* winter?"

The days snailed by. It was dark a lot and it

was damp and everything seemed grey, grey, grey. Jim stamped about. His sister came home with a plastic thermometer and a clipboard and started measuring air temperature for her project. "Fifteen degrees in the broom cupboard," she announced smugly. "Five degrees by the window," scribble scribble. "Two degrees below freezing outside the front door."

It was eight degrees below the next morning and everything was greyer than ever. The whole street seemed frozen and gloomy, with the cars and buses swishing by as if there were nobody inside them and the tall houses crowded together in two long, hard-faced rows, their doors shut and their curtains drawn against the cold.

"With so many people living in one street you'd think there'd be something interesting going on or somebody friendly to talk to," said Jim to Arthur as they stomped to school puffing steam. But the passers-by just hurried on with their collars up and their faces closed. That was the day the school heating broke down and they were sent home for the rest of the week. Jim was very bored.

Then next morning he woke up to a strange sound. The sound was strange because it wasn't there – everything was quiet. It was so quiet that Jim thought he'd better go back to sleep. If the street wasn't roaring with traffic it couldn't be time to get up yet. He scrunched his head back into the pillow and closed his eyes again. Then he realized it was light, and a strange, bright light too. And if it was light already it had to be well past time to get up.

Jim rolled out of bed on to his feet and stumbled over to the window. He froze his fingers rubbing a clear place in the frost patterns on the glass, and then he saw it.

"It's snowing," he shouted, and ran across the landing into his sister's room. "Look, Lizzie! It's snowed and it's snowing, it's snowing and it's snowed!"

Lizzie grunted and buried her head under the covers.

Jim bounced downstairs. "It's snowed 'n' it's snowing 'n' it's snowing 'n' it's snowed 'n' it's..."

The cat ignored him with a pained look and his mum seemed to be more interested in his feet than the weather.

"I know, I know," she said, putting herself firmly between him and the front door. "But it's freezing out there and you haven't even got your slippers on."

"Snow snow snow snow," chanted Jim all the way back up the stairs and into his clothes all inside out and anyhow.

"Snooooooooooooow," he sang as he slid back down the banisters.

"I'm going out," he told his mum.

"Well, at least have something hot first," she said.

Then they heard the first thump. It was a bit muffled but it was definitely a thump.

"I wonder what that was?" said his mum and stopped trying to wiggle her bit of burnt toast out of the toaster.

Jim was at the front door and out before anyone could stop him.

Crunch!

Outside, the whole world was strange and white, and great noiseless flakes of snow floated unhurriedly down. Jim stared in amazement.

His house was on a hill, and just where it stood the street tipped round a bit of a bend, not that you'd really notice it most of the time. Now everything was covered with snow: chimneys, roofs, trees, walls, railings, bins, parked cars and of course the pavement and the road itself. They were all transformed – soft, white and rounded. All except for one thing that is.

For there, just below the bend, was a big shiny blue car with scarcely a flake of snow on it. It had obviously spent the night in a garage, but now it was slewed across the road and stuck nose first into a pillow of snow that was the back of a parked van.

Jim could see silvery skid marks in the snow and two great curves where the back wheels of the blue car had swung round into the middle of the road when it hit the van.

He also recognized the bits of red metal tangled up with the blue as the back of a van belonging to Ken from two doors down. This should be interesting, he thought to himself, kicking up a flurry of snow.

The driver of the blue car was getting out. He walked round to the dent that used to be the front of his car and watched the hot water pouring out of its smashed radiator in disbelief. It was very quiet.

Jim tried some skidding himself. His trainers were brilliant. They ploughed down the pavement filling to the brims with snow.

"Whee!" crowed Jim, dancing in his tracks. "I'm the first man on the moon!" He stretched out his arms and watched his bright red sweatshirt become speckled with white.

Then a door slammed and Ken, who owned the van, came storming out of his house and across the road. He was still wearing his dressing-gown, and the pair of wellington boots he'd put on underneath made him look like an angry Father Christmas. He and the man from the blue car started waving their arms at each other while the leaking radiator melted a hot, black patch into the snow carpet and the car stayed blocking the road.

Jim watched from a safe distance and drew stick figures on the window of a car parked in front of his house.

By the time the twenty-to-eight bus came up the road the other way there were two cars waiting to get down past the crash, and Ken and the man from the blue car had given up trying to prize the two vehicles apart and were scribbling on bits of paper. Jim saw the bus first. He jumped up and down and waved his arms. But it was too late.

The bus driver braked, and with a sigh the great double decker slid silently across the snowy road and thumped into the other side of the blue car. Crunch!

The passengers on the bus looked surprised to find themselves facing straight into the front room of number sixty-two. The driver scratched her head. But the man from the

blue car looked
as if he was
about to
pop.

"Can't you look where you're going, you silly cow?" he shrieked. "You shouldn't be in charge of a public vehicle if you can't keep control of it..." On and on he went, but just as it was slowly but surely swallowing up his car, the falling snow seemed to swallow up his words too, until the man reminded Jim of nothing so much as a goldfish silently opening and shutting its mouth.

"Jim! Just look at you! You haven't even got your boots on!" said his mum, suddenly appearing beside him and steering him firmly back towards the house. "Now, you have some breakfast while I go and see if anyone's hurt."

Jim was hungry, his trainers were soaked and he couldn't feel anything where his toes were supposed to be. He decided it would be quicker to eat than to argue.

He shook the snow out of his hair, squelched off his shoes and started to gobble some cereal at record speed. How could Lizzie go on sleeping on a day like this, even if there weren't any school? he marvelled, banging a piece of bread into the toaster. He wasn't going to waste his winter. He had plans. There was a giant snowman for the back yard and then a snowball fight with Arthur… He watched absently as a plume of smoke started to rise from the toaster… Maybe they could go to the park – it had some great hills for sliding down. Pity they didn't have a sledge.

The smoke got blacker.

Jim sighed and gave up. He unplugged the toaster, turned it upside down and shook it till not only the little lump of charcoal that was his toast, but the whole electrical insides came out too.

"Oh, dear," he said.

Just then there was another thump.

And another.

A Nice Cup of Tea

By the time Jim got back outside there was a scramble of tangled cars in the road. A green builder's van had skidded into the car behind the car behind the bus and pushed them all into a giant zigzag. And from up the hill a flashy silver sports car had skated down, tipped the milkman's float over into the gutter and tried to climb into the boot of the car in front.

It was quite a sight – a heap of crumpled machines, still and mostly silent except for a bit of hissing here and dripping there, with the snow, taking no notice of any of it, falling like Christmas decorations.

What a lot of people, thought Jim.

The neighbours had all come out to see, and for the first time in ages the street looked really lived-in. There was Mrs Edwards from across the way, still in her slippers –

Jim didn't usually see much of her – and Dave, the milkman, on his hands and knees trying to collect up some of the milk bottles and cartons of juice from the piles of snow where they had landed. The passengers from the bus and the drivers of the cars were all standing around gaping and exclaiming. And apart from the driver of the silver car, whose nosebleed was dripping red splashes on to the snow, nobody seemed to be hurt.

But the road was blocked.

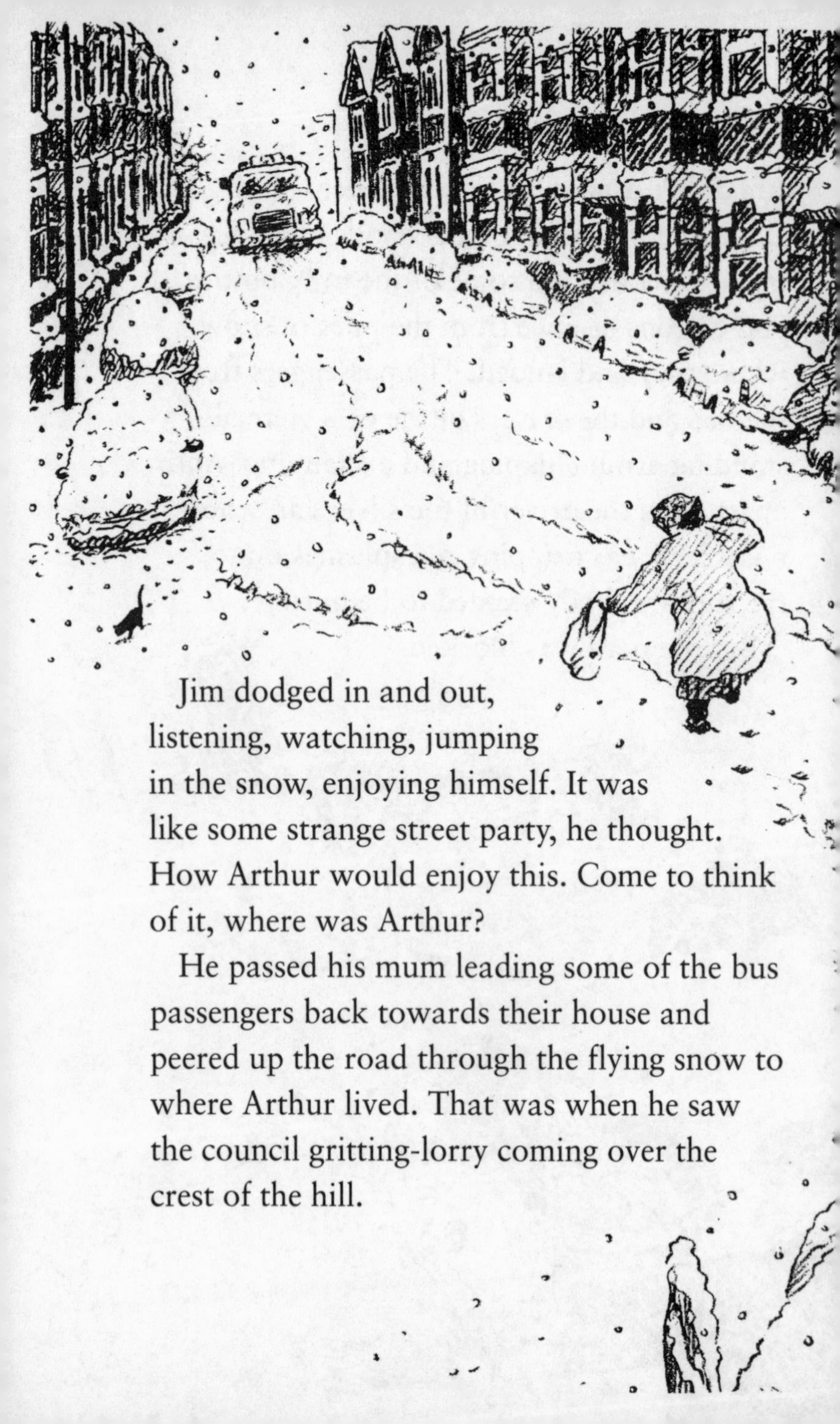

Jim dodged in and out, listening, watching, jumping in the snow, enjoying himself. It was like some strange street party, he thought. How Arthur would enjoy this. Come to think of it, where was Arthur?

He passed his mum leading some of the bus passengers back towards their house and peered up the road through the flying snow to where Arthur lived. That was when he saw the council gritting-lorry coming over the crest of the hill.

It was big and yellow and battered. The orange light on its roof was flashing and the spinning bit at the back was flinging grit in all directions. The only problem was that there weren't many directions left: straight ahead was the tangle of crashed cars blocking the way; on either side was the kerb lined with the white mounds that were parked cars; and behind the lorry itself came a queue of other cars. There was no escape.

The grit bounced off the parked and not-so-parked cars, chipping little bits of paint off and scattering them in the snow as the lorry rolled on. The roar of its engine got louder and louder. Everybody turned to watch. Would it or wouldn't it stop in time?

The lorry shuddered and slowed and then, like something in a slow-motion film, it glided smoothly down the wrong side of the road and came to a standstill just a few centimetres away from the milk float. The driver stuck out his hairy head, topped with a red bobble hat, and grinned. "Well, well, well. Who's been being clever here then?" he said.

He wasn't grinning quite so much a few minutes later when he tried to reverse his lorry back up the road and found the front wheels would only spin on the spot.

"Better make the best of a bad job," said Mrs Edwards, hurrying past with a tray and still in her pink fluffy slippers. "Have a nice hot mug of tea," she said, handing him one.

“I’d like an extra two pints of milk please, dear,” she said to the milkman, or what she could see of him sticking out from under a parked car, where he was searching for his lost bottles. “And you, James, you can be helpful and carry the sugar bowl and spoon for me,” she added, turning to Jim.

Jim hated being called James.

“Aren’t your feet cold?” he asked, staring at her snow-caked slippers.

Jim felt a bit stupid standing about with the sugar bowl once Mrs Edwards had gone back indoors to make a fresh pot of tea.

He was just carefully putting it down in the cushion of snow on top of her gatepost when something hit him on the back of his head and he felt snow slithering down his neck like icy fingers on his skin.

He spun round just in time to see Arthur duck down behind the snow-coated mound of a car on the other side of the street.

"I'll get you!" Jim shouted, as the icy fingers slithered further down inside his shirt, and, scooping up his own handful of snow, he squodged it into a ball and hurled it at Arthur.

Jim had never been very good at throwing. Now he had cold hands too. He missed Arthur. He even missed the parked car. Instead he got the milkman, who had just emerged from his snowdrift and was offering round orange juice from a damaged carton.

"Sorry!" yelled Jim, as a fine orange splash spread out across the snow. For a moment the milkman looked distinctly puzzled. He screwed up his eyes and scanned the street through the falling snow until he saw Jim. Then he grinned and, bending down, made his own snowball, white with orange streaks like some fancy ice-cream.

Jim dodged. The snowball came flying across the street, gently tickled the pale-blue curls of Mrs Edwards, who was on her way out with the fresh tea, and exploded against the wall of her house.

Oh, no! thought Jim. This gets worse and worse!

He turned anxiously to try and explain, expecting to find Mrs Edwards shocked and upset. But it was Jim who was surprised. Mrs Edwards wasn't the least bit upset. She wasn't raging. She wasn't even shaking. Far from it. She just bent down, parked the teapot behind the dustbins and calmly set to work.

"Oh, I had lots of practice when I was young, dear," she said to Jim, noticing his surprise as she hurtled her first snowball over the gate. "We had good winters then. Lots of this stuff." She scooped enthusiastically. "It's been years since I had the chance of a good snowball fight!" She lobbed another and another, and before long she had let a whole volley of snowballs loose on the world beyond her gate.

Jim was full of admiration. Her aim was

brilliant. Her speed incredible. If only he could throw like that.

Arthur and the milkman were not so pleased. Scurrying for cover behind the tangle of cars in the road, they tried to keep up with Mrs Edwards, but even with two of them it was a struggle.

Jim peered out from behind the bins where he was crouching next to the teapot, and chuckled. The next moment he saw one of Mrs Edwards's snowballs fly off in an odd direction. Instead of heading for the milkman it flew straight at the grit-lorry man, who was standing chatting on the pavement, and caught him smack on the seat of his trousers. The grit-man jumped and Mrs Edwards winked gleefully at Jim.

"Well, it's no fun if you aim all the time, is it?"

That did it. Now everyone joined in, the grit-man, the drivers and the remaining bus passengers; even Jim came out from behind the bins, and for a glorious few minutes there were snowballs flying and snowflakes flurrying everywhere in a great white carnival of snow and laughter. It was as if winter had taken over and nothing else mattered.

But one driver was still sitting doggedly inside his snowbound car, trying to talk on his car phone. As the din outside got louder and louder, so he got crosser and crosser until at last he wound down his window in a fury and opened his mouth to shout... And just then, a perfectly-timed snowball landed on the edge of the wound-down window and exploded in his face.

"Blooming kids!" spluttered the man, glowering in Jim's direction. "Useless layabouts! I'll sort you out once and for all!" and he made to get out of his car.

But Mrs Edwards wasn't having that. Oh no!

With a single commanding gesture of her hand she stopped the snowball fight. Then she put down her latest snowball, picked up the teapot and advanced into the road. The snow-caked motorist was struggling with his seat-belt and roaring with rage.

"That's quite enough of that, young man," said Mrs Edwards firmly. "Now stop being silly and calm down this minute."

The motorist
stared in disbelief
at this little old woman with blue hair and pink slippers, who was standing in the snow telling him off.

"Besides, I don't think you're supposed to park in the middle of the road, are you?"

The motorist groaned and banged his damp car phone back into its holder.

"That's a good boy," said Mrs Edwards soothingly. "Now what you need is a nice cup of tea."

And with that she took a teacup out of her pocket, filled it from the rapidly-cooling teapot and handed it to him. The grit-man, the milkman, Arthur, and all the others laughed and cheered.

Mrs Edwards turned on her pink fluffy heel to go home.

"And now, if you'll excuse me, I have my work to do. James, offer the gentleman some sugar!"

The Giant Skid Slide

Jim joined Arthur at last and together they wandered down the hill. The snow was still falling and gradually even the bus and the crumpled cars were being turned into smooth white shapes that looked as if they'd always been there. Nothing moved.

"My dad says it's going to take them ages to clear the road, 'specially now the gritting-lorry's stuck," said Arthur. "And look at all those cars waiting." He stared at the frozen traffic.

But Jim had tipped his head back and was gazing up at the sky with his mouth open. The falling flakes looked dark against the grey-white clouds above. That's odd, thought Jim, when they look so white on the ground. A snowflake landed on his tongue and melted so fast he couldn't even taste it.

"I wish I'd got out here sooner," went on Arthur. "It must have been amazing with all those cars skidding and sliding all over the place."

Jim closed his mouth and tipped his head

forward into its normal position. He ran down a bit further and did a little skid.

"It was the blue car that started it," he called to Arthur over his shoulder. "It went on for miles..."

He ran a bit and then did another long skid. Arthur ran after him.

"Wheeee!" he shouted.

"As for the bus..." said Jim, stretching out his arms and spinning round on his heel.

"Thump!" said Arthur, bumping into him.

"Exactly," said Jim.

The snow gently decorated the two boys as they skipped and skidded and slid down the empty pavement. It was as if they had the whole city to themselves.

"I saw the grit-lorry though," said Arthur. "Look out! Here I come!"

Putting his head down and whirling his arms round and round like the grit-spreader, Arthur powered down towards Jim.

His feet ploughed fresh tracks through the untouched snow and threw up a soft white shower on either side. Then he hit the track of Jim's last skid. Faster and faster he went, his arms flailing in earnest now. He teetered, he tottered, then his feet shot out from under him and he landed with a thump.

"That was really fast!" said Jim with admiration. "Are you all right?"

There was a pause while Arthur got his breath back.

"It wasn't just fast, it was brilliant!" said Arthur, patting the snow beside him. "It was your skid that did it. It made the pavement all smooth, like glass." He brushed snow out of his eyes and picked out some more from inside his jacket. Then he stopped. "Hey, we could make a proper track you know, like those bob-sleigh runs on television. Then we could go really fast! All we'd have to do is smooth the snow down." He patted the snow again.

Jim crouched down beside him. "And we could polish it and make it extra slippery..." He jumped up again. "We could make a skid slide, a really long one." Jim danced around in the falling snow and Arthur grinned.

"Yeah!" he cheered.

"All right," said Jim. "You do this bit. I'll do the next bit down." And he skidded away down the pavement and set to work.

It was wonderfully peaceful down there on the ground, curtained in falling snow. Not a car could be heard, the road was quite still and Jim was soon completely absorbed in building his section of the Giant Skid Slide.

The snow was extraordinary – you could

build it and bend it into all sorts of strange, cold curves. Jim shaped and he moulded, he stroked and he smoothed, he even took off his jacket and polished the gleaming track. This is more like it, he thought to himself. This is what life should be like!

A cracked voice startled him.

"I don't know!" it muttered crossly from somewhere very close. Jim spun round, shocked by the sudden sound, and looked up. There on the edge of the front path nearest to him towered a huge gaunt figure in a flapping black cloak, like some great carrion crow.

For a moment Jim held his breath. He stared up, half blinded by the whiteness. Then slowly he realized that this looming shape was really just a bony old man in a shabby black overcoat and scarf, balancing gingerly on two sticks.

"I don't know," said the voice again. "You youngsters are turning the pavement into a skating rink. How am I supposed to walk

on this?" and he pointed shakily at Jim's masterpiece with one of his sticks.

It was old Mr O'Connor from number seventy-three. Not that Jim really knew him or anything. His mum went in to see him from time to time because he lived alone, but Jim had never been. In fact he couldn't ever

remember hearing Mr O'Connor talk before. He'd seen him often enough though, scowling through his torn net curtains when they were playing in the street, or shuffling along the pavement, muttering silently to himself. He looked old and bony and cross and Jim was scared of him.

"Er ... sorry," he said, backing away. "I didn't think ... er ... we were only ... I'm sorry."

"The milk hasn't even come yet," Mr O'Connor went on, "and I don't know how I'm going to go and get it."

"Milk," echoed Jim, wondering frantically how to escape. "Oh, dear... No milk." Then, as if he'd only just learnt the word, "Ah, *milk*! Don't worry," he shouted with relief, "I can get that." And he ran off up the road towards the overturned milk float as if the hounds of hell were after him.

The old man stood there unsteadily with the snow whirling gently around him and followed the boy with his eyes. He didn't have long to wait.

"Here you are," Jim was saying a few minutes later. "One bottle of silver-top milk." He held out the bottle to the gaunt figure and hoped and prayed he could get away now.

But Mr O'Connor didn't take it.

Jim stopped peering round to see where Arthur had got to and looked more carefully at the old man. Seen from close to, he didn't look so big any more. Jim's eyes took in the spindly, thin legs, the icy path and the knotted hands grasping the two walking sticks, and then, as if in a dream, he heard himself say, "Would you like me to take the milk indoors for you?"

Into the Darkness

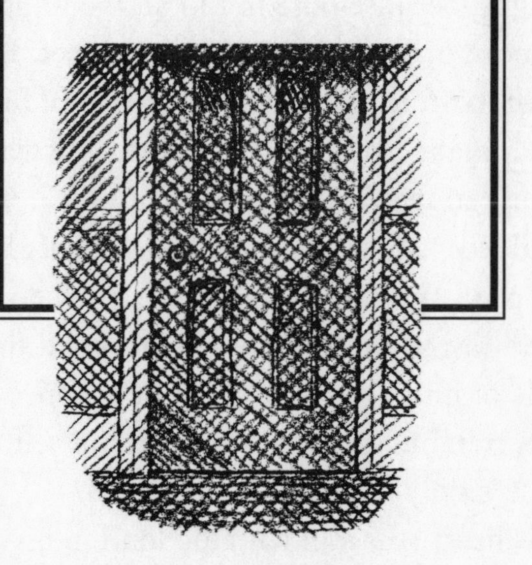

Jim opened the front door of number seventy-three. Mr O'Connor's house was very dark after the brightness outside. It smelt funny too, and it was cold, really cold. Jim had never been in there before. He felt his way along in the darkness and it felt like crawling into a tunnel.

The kitchen must be at the back, he thought, because ours is and all the houses are more or less the same in this street. But this didn't feel at all like home. It could have been a place from another planet. He was starting to feel frightened.

Suddenly something brushed past his legs at top speed and bolted out of the front door. It scared Jim so much he nearly dropped the bottle of milk. For a moment he stopped dead, trembling. Then he forced himself to go on. "It's only the cat," he muttered.

His heart was still banging loud in his chest when in the gloom he saw something else, something moving in the air, twisting and writhing towards him, almost like a ghost.

He stumbled and lurched sideways. Somehow he'd reached the end of the hall and banged into a door where there wasn't a door in his house. That was real enough.

As the door swung open, Jim saw a reddish shape flicker on the floor beyond. He saw it leap up as the air from the hall rushed in, lighting up other twisting, trailing shadows, shadows rushing towards him from the room beyond, shadows with an unmistakable smell.

Ghosts? No, Jim knew they weren't ghosts now. This was smoke, thick smoke, and even as he looked the redness turned to tongues of flame and licked at the floor of the kitchen.

Jim raced back down the dark hall and out of the front door. He nearly knocked Mr O'Connor over as he skidded out on to the path, pale as a ghost himself.

"Fire!" he shouted. "Your kitchen's on fire! We've got to call the fire brigade!"

Mr O'Connor looked bewildered. "What?" he said. "What's that? What's happened?"

A wisp of smoke followed Jim out of the front door. He knew there was no time to waste. "Stay there, Mr O'Connor!" he shouted as he turned to go. "Don't try and go in! There's a fire! FIRE! I'm going to get help." He raced out of the gate and up the road, his feet slithering and sliding and the snowflakes stinging his face like little needles of fear.

Help!

Jim crashed blindly through the front door of his own house, scattering the shoes and boots lined up in the hall and showering snow everywhere.

The air in the house was warm, and a clink of cups and the peaceful buzz of conversation came from the front room where some of the bus passengers and car drivers were still having tea. Jim burst in like an explosion of winter.

"Mum!"

he shouted, as if she'd never hear him and then, as he saw his mother's eyes swing down to his boots already melting snow into the carpet, "No, Mum! Fire, Mum! Mr O'Connor's kitchen's on fire. We've got to get help!"

There was a sudden silence and then a buzz of excited talk and tut-tutting from the grown-ups sitting around. Suddenly Jim felt like crying. Was anyone ever going to listen?

But his mum wasn't tut-tutting. She was right in front of him, looking straight into his face and listening hard.

"Come on," she said, when he finished, "I'll ring the fire brigade."

Jim hovered anxiously on the doorstep while his mother dialled 999. It seemed to take for ever, as if time had come to a standstill. His heart was pounding and inside his head he saw again the dragons' tongues of flame licking hungrily at Mr O'Connor's kitchen.

The quiet, white, winter world he stared out at seemed strange, unreal. There was the empty bus jammed across the road. There was the blue car, now almost white. There were the other scrunched and tangled cars, a frozen traffic jam stretching back in both directions up and down the hill. And there was the snow, still peacefully but relentlessly falling.

And Jim's heart froze.

Of course! How could they be so stupid? The road was blocked! How was a fire engine ever going to reach number seventy-three, even if it got as far as the end of the road without skidding like the bus or getting stuck like the gritting-lorry? What on earth were they going to do?

A cold, scared feeling ran down the back of Jim's neck and clawed at his back.

He shivered. And then Arthur came up the path towards him, calling, "What's the matter with you? You ran right past me!"

Whether it was the icy feeling down his neck or Arthur's face that did it Jim couldn't be sure, but it was then he had his brilliant idea. In a split second he realized that there was one thing they could do, a strange thing... It would take a miracle, but it might work, if only they could move fast enough.

Suddenly Jim was in a fever – explaining to Arthur, explaining to his mum, explaining to Lizzie, who had just appeared, tousle-headed and half asleep. Then he was running, running back down the road. And behind him the fever spread.

Lizzie rushed off upstairs to get dressed. Arthur went tearing across the street to get Mrs Edwards and Jim's mother threw open the door of the front room and, herding the buzzing tea-drinkers out of their comfortable chairs and into their coats and boots, she swept them out of the house and down the road.

Back at number seventy-three the smoke was drifting sleepily out of the open front door and starting to blacken the snow by the time they arrived. Mr O'Connor looked small and shaky standing there. Jim couldn't remember why the old man had seemed so scary before. "I can't have put the guard up," he said again and again. "It must have been a coal jumped out of the fire."

"Don't you worry," said the grit-man, putting a huge arm round his shoulder, "we're all here to help now."

And so they were. There was quite a crowd: the drivers from the cars, the grit-man and the milkman, the bus passengers and the neighbours – even Lizzie with her pyjama top hanging out from under her anorak. And here was Arthur with Mrs Edwards at last.

"Well, young James," she said, "I hear you've got a plan. Let's have it then."

The Greatest Snowball Fight Ever

It looked as
if they'd all gone
mad. There were the
snowflakes floating slowly
down. There was the road,
blocked with bent and stuck
cars. There was the grimy smoke
creeping out of Mr O'Connor's doorway.
And what were the people doing? They were
down on their hands and knees, frantically
scooping and clutching at the snow.

They swept it off the car roofs and grabbed it up out of the gutters. They packed it and scrunched it and made it into lumps, and then from all sides they passed it – one huge lump of snow after another – from hand to hand along the line to the door of number seventy-three.

Jim and his mother piled them up on the step, and Jim's mum passed them to the milkman in the hall, and the

milkman in the hall passed them through the dingy smoke to Mrs Edwards and the grit-man by the kitchen door, dishcloths tied across their noses and mouths to stop the smoke, looking for all the world like a pair of bandits in the darkness.

And the bandits threw them. Into the thickening smoke and the flames beyond, one after another they threw the snowballs crashing and hissing into Mr O'Connor's burning kitchen. They threw with both hands. They threw as if they had eight arms each. They threw until they almost fell over with exhaustion. It was the greatest snowball fight ever.

The fire didn't like it. It sizzled and it hissed. It shot little flames up in odd places and then disappeared again. It sulked and it smoked and it started to shrink.

They changed places. Other people took their turn at the front of the chain and gave Mrs Edwards and the grit-man a chance to cough and rub the smoke out of their streaming eyes outside. Slowly they seemed to be winning. A stream of dirty water was trickling out of the hall door and inside the flames had disappeared, but smoke was still coming from the place where Jim had first seen it.

"We need something really big to smother it with," said Mrs Edwards.

"Look out!" It was Arthur tearing down the pavement, scattering people to either side as he came. "Look out. Make way!"

Through the whiteness up the road they could just see Lizzie pushing something big, and not just big but getting bigger. It was a giant snowball.

"Brilliant!" said Jim, as it came rolling on down the hill, leaving a bare trail behind it as it picked up the snow from the pavement. It was bumping steadily along now,

didn't need much pushing, gathering speed. Now it had left Lizzie behind. It was almost at number seventy-three.

"Come on, everybody!" shouted Jim.

It was just then that the man from the fire brigade arrived, looking worried. "I'm sorry it's taken us so long," he said. "We've had a bit of a problem with..."

"Catch it!" yelled Arthur.

"What?" asked the man.

The snowball didn't really run into him. It just sort of nudged into his legs from behind, but it was enough to slide his feet out from under him. The man from the fire brigade landed with a bump on the pavement, turning the snowball round the corner and on to Mr O'Connor's front path. There was a cheer and everyone rushed to heave it along the path, through the front door of the house and into the darkness.

There was a soggy crash and then silence.

Everyone stared anxiously towards the dark doorway of number seventy-three.

Slowly, slowly, the smoke in the passageway thinned and then cleared to show Jim and Mrs Edwards coming out waving and grinning.

"We've done it!" coughed Jim, running up to Mr O'Connor and beaming at him in his excitement. "It's a miracle! It's going to be all right!"

And, like a second miracle, the old man looked up at him and smiled back.

By the time the cheering had died down, the other firemen had trudged their way up the road to number seventy-three. They spent the rest of the day clearing up and making sure the building was safe and that the fire wasn't going to break out again. They said they were very impressed. They didn't usually like people to tackle fires themselves, but it was lucky that someone had moved fast today or the whole house would have burnt down.

Gradually, people said goodbye and went back to their homes to get out of the snow. Jim's mum took Mr O'Connor to their house to warm up and recover from the shock. Jim and Arthur stayed to watch.

The firemen cleared out what was left of Mr O'Connor's kitchen and piled the remains – the contents of his cupboards, the bits of lino and the charred kitchen furniture – in a blackened heap outside the front door of number seventy-three. The heap steamed and the falling snowflakes melted with a hiss.

Late in the afternoon when Jim and Arthur

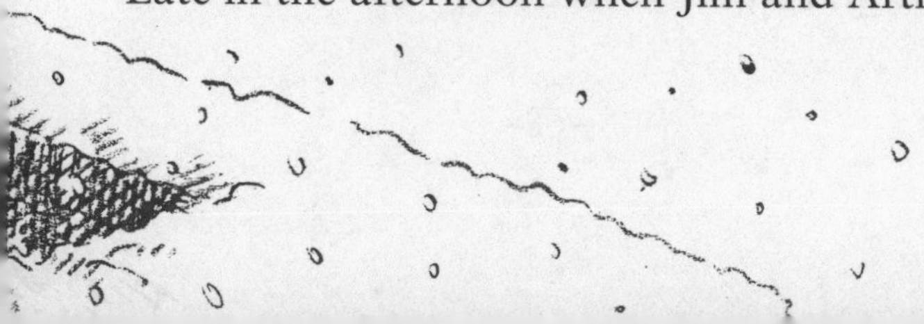

finally left, the men were still working, emptying the cellar beneath the kitchen, just to make sure there was nothing smouldering there. The house looked bleak and wrecked and it was bitterly cold.

"Old people can die of cold you know," said Jim's mum later that evening, as she helped Jim move his things out of his own room and into Lizzie's. "And you won't mind sharing with Lizzie for a while will you?"

Jim pulled a face.

"Mr O'Connor's a nice old man," she said, ignoring him, then she smiled. "He reminds me of my grandad you know, and you wouldn't believe what wonderful stories he used to tell us. It's a pity you never knew him. Yes, it'll do us good to have a man –" she stopped and looked at Jim – "I mean a grown-up man, in the house again for a while." Jim sighed. "Besides," and she waved her hand at the icy darkness outside, "you wouldn't want to turn anyone out in this weather would you?"

Jim stared out of the window. *He* wouldn't mind being out there he thought sleepily. The snow had almost stopped falling now and the sky above was clear and black and spiked with hundreds of brilliant stars. He'd never seen them so bright before. Outside his bedroom window a long icicle was hanging from the gutter – it looked sharp – and, beyond, the street and the houses were wrapped in a soft white muffler of snow and glowed in the street light.

Jim yawned. Winter was certainly strange and powerful to be able to change everything so much. And it wasn't just the world outside that had changed either, he thought ruefully. Yesterday the world might have been grey and boring, but at least he'd been able to go to sleep in his own bed. Now here he was moving to the spare bed in Lizzie's room so that an old man he'd never even spoken to before this morning could have his room, his own precious room.

Jim sighed and tried to feel indignant, but for some reason he didn't mind as much as he thought he ought to.

His mum gave him a hug. "Don't you worry. Mr O'Connor will only be staying for a little while, until his house is fixed up again. And by the way," she tipped Jim's chin up towards her and looked into his eyes, "I'm very proud of you, you know." There was a pause, then she grinned, "So come on, let's get this over with and then you can go to bed."

Jim was too tired to argue, too tired even to tease Lizzie. He fell asleep like someone falling into a great soft snowdrift.

Not Quite the Same

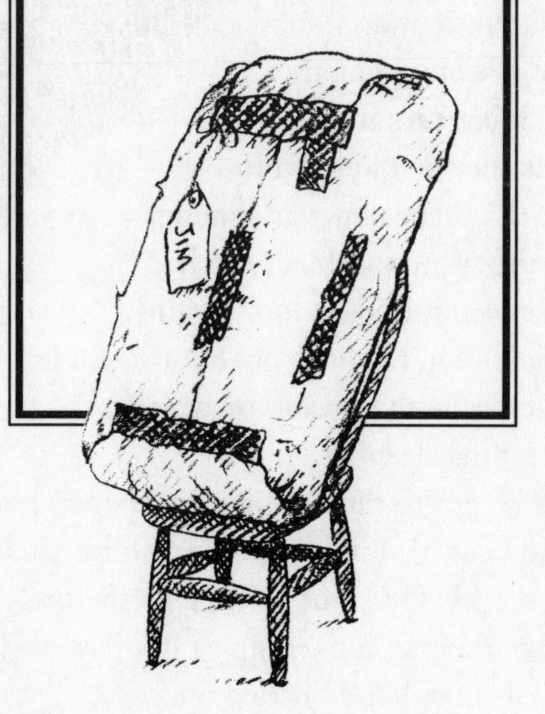

Next morning
Jim was woken
by the clanking
of chains and the
groaning of metal.
The tow trucks
had arrived and
were disentangling the
remaining cars from the
knots they'd skidded into
yesterday. The sun was shining
and the snow sparkled. Jim had
never seen the street look so fine.

He couldn't wait to get out there. He was cross with himself for wasting so much time sleeping.

As he got to the bottom of the stairs he could hear his mum humming in the kitchen and see Mr O'Connor sitting by the fire.

The old man looked up as Jim passed. Jim sort of smiled and hurried on.

"I'm just going out, Mum," he called as he reached the front door.

"Come and have some breakfast first!"
She sounded firm.
"Oh, must I?" he groaned.
"Yes." It wasn't worth
arguing with that
tone of voice.

Jim headed into the kitchen and dived for the table. Then he stopped. There on his chair was a huge, brown paper parcel with his name on it.

"What's this, Mum?"

"Hmm," said his mum vaguely. "Why don't you open it?"

Jim prodded at the parcel and started to undo the brown paper. Underneath there was newspaper, a great thick layer of it, and inside the newspaper was what looked like an old piece of greying wood. Jim ripped off the last of the wrapping and pulled the wood out.

"Oh, wow!" he yelled. "A sledge! Mum, it's brilliant!"

He turned over the long wooden shape and felt the runners. It was big and strong and he'd never seen one like it before. His mother smiled. "It's nothing to do with me," she said. "That's a present from Mr O'Connor."

Jim was speechless. He turned round, sort of ashamed and embarrassed.

The old man was looking at him, and his eyes were anxious.

There was a silence.

Then Jim managed, “Er … thank you.”

The old man nodded.

“I made it for my lad when he was a youngster,” he said with an effort.

Jim looked at it again. “Did you really?” he said, admiring. “It’s great!”

There was another silence.

“The firemen found it when they cleared the cellar last night… I thought you might like it.” Mr O’Connor paused, as if he wasn’t used to so much talking.

"Oh, yes!" said Jim. "*Yes, please!*"

The old man's face had relaxed, softened. He even looks quite friendly, thought Jim. Mr O'Connor mumbled something.

"Pardon?" said Jim.

"For your help yesterday, for lending me your room … thank you."

"Oh, that's all right," Jim heard himself saying. "That's quite all right."

And maybe it was.

His mother handed him a bacon sandwich and stuffed an apple in his pocket.

"I expect you want to be getting out there don't you? Go on, off you go now." She gave him a push.

"Oh, *thanks,* Mum." Jim picked up the old sledge and patted it proudly. "I can't wait to show this to Arthur." And he ran out of the room.

A minute later, coat and boots and hat on, he came back into the room.

"See you later, Mr O'Connor," he said. The old man smiled one of his rare smiles.

Jim and Arthur sledged and sledged all day long, up and down the hills in the sparkling winter park. The old sledge was hard and heavy and very fast. It flew down the slopes like a bird and they flew with it.

By the time they came home they were tired and soaked and cold and very happy, and the world was showing signs of changing back to normal.

All around, the city was breaking back through its white winter cloak. Patches of salt and grit, sweet wrappers and newspapers had appeared on the snowy pavements; snow had slipped off roofs here and there; grey tarmac had returned to the middle of the roads and the wheels of the buses threw spurts of brown slush in all directions.

The silence had gone – the traffic roared again.

Even the school heating had been fixed Arthur's mum told them, when they got back to his house. The boys groaned. It would be back to school tomorrow.

Jim said goodbye to Arthur and headed for home, pulling the sledge behind him. Soon there'd be nothing left, he thought, as he kicked his way through the churned-up snow on the pavement. In a few days time everything would be just the same as before.

"Hello, James," called Mrs Edwards from the other side of the street. "Don't forget to pop in sometime," and she grinned at him.

He waved and the sledge tugged at his hand. Well, maybe not quite the same, thought Jim.